ARTEMIS, THE ARCHER GODDESS

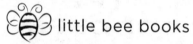 little bee books

New York, NY
Copyright © 2022 by Little Bee Books
All rights reserved, including the right of reproduction in whole or in part in any form.
Manufactured in China RRD 0921
littlebeebooks.com

Library of Congress Cataloging-in-Publication Data is available upon request.
ISBN: 978-1-4998-1155-1 (hc)
First Edition 10 9 8 7 6 5 4 3 2 1
ISBN: 978-1-4998-1156-8 (pbk)
First Edition 10 9 8 7 6 5 4 3 2 1
ISBN: 978-1-4998-1238-1 (ebook)

For information about special discounts on bulk purchases, please contact Little Bee Books at sales@littlebeebooks.com.

BOOK 4

Little Olympians

ARTEMIS, THE ARCHER GODDESS

BY A.I. NEWTON   ILLUSTRATED BY ANJAN SARKAR

little bee books

TABLE OF CONTENTS

THE GODS OF OLYMPUS

Once, all-powerful gods ruled from their home atop the cloud-covered heights of Mount Olympus. Zeus, God of Thunder; Athena, Goddess of Wisdom; Apollo, the Sun God; Ares, God of Combat; Aphrodite, Goddess of Beauty and Nature; Poseidon, God of the Seas; Artemis, Goddess of the Hunt; and others possessed incredible powers, and controlled the fate of humans on Earth...

1

...but these powerful beings were not always the mighty Gods of Olympus. Once, long ago, they were just a bunch of kids...

2

BIG NEWS!

Artemis and Athena stared at the game in front of them. They were concentrating hard as they played petteia, a very complicated board game. Athena was the current petteia champion at Camp Eureka.

Artemis really wanted to beat her.

Poseidon, their mentor and counselor at Eureka, where the young gods were learning to use their great powers, had given his students some time off. They were enjoying a bit of relaxation following their recent intense studies, travels, and adventures.

Artemis and Athena sat on stone seats and leaned over the petteia board. A group of their fellow young gods had gathered around to watch them play.

Aphrodite loved analyzing the various strategies needed to win petteia. She leaned over and watched as Artemis focused intently on her next move.

"If you concentrate any harder, I think you're going to stare a hole right through the game board," Aphrodite joked.

Artemis said nothing and continued to study the board.

Nearby, Apollo and Ares leaned over a thick, sawed-off tree trunk. They were arm wrestling, as Zeus and Hermes looked on.

Their arm muscles bulged. Their teeth clenched as veins began to pop out of their necks. Their fingers started to turn purple. Yet, so far, neither could budge the other's arm.

"I think the object is to actually move the other guy's arm," Hermes said to his two struggling friends.

But Apollo and Ares were working much too hard to reply.

"It's great to have a little time off," Zeus said to Hermes as they watched the mighty contest. "Poseidon has been training us nonstop since we got to Eureka. We've done so much, it's kind of hard to remember it all. I know that my parents are going to want to hear about *everything* that happened."

Hermes smiled a mischievous smile. "Well, then why don't we tell them!"

Zeus looked confused. "What do you mean?" he asked.

"I think we should start a newspaper," Hermes said, getting very excited by the idea. "We could report on all our accomplishments and everything that happens here. Then we could circulate it around the camp and share it with our families back home, too. I know that my parents would sure be proud of my heroic run that saved the city of Argos!"

"Gotcha!" Ares shouted, finally pinning Apollo's arm to the top of the tree stump.

"No fair!" Apollo complained. "My elbow slipped."

"And who wouldn't want to read about Ares's big arm wrestling win, or Apollo's excuses and whining about losing?" Hermes continued.

At that moment, Artemis and Athena joined the others, having finished their game. "What are you two talking about?"

"I'm going to start a newspaper to cover all the important events here at Eureka," Hermes explained.

"Well, I have your first headline," said Artemis, raising her hands. "Artemis is Camp Eureka's new petteia champion after beating Athena!"

Athena smiled, taking her loss in stride. "Well, that *is* big news," she said.

"That's it!" Hermes cried. "I'll call the newspaper . . . the *Eureka News*. I better get to work on the first issue!"

CHAPTER 2

NEWSWORTHY CONTESTS

Excitement about Hermes's newspaper spread throughout the camp.

"*My* achievement is going to be the first headline," boasted Apollo.

"Achievement at what?" asked Athena.

"I haven't figured that out yet," Apollo replied, shrugging his shoulders.

"I have an idea," said Hermes. "Why don't we set up some games for all of us to play, then I can cover those in the *Eureka News*."

"Great idea!" said Apollo. "The sooner you have something to write about, the sooner I'll be the front page headline."

Artemis rolled her eyes at her brother, but remained silent.

The young gods got busy planning a series of informal competitions.

After some discussion, Athena and Aphrodite agreed to a rock climbing contest. They were going to scale a rocky cliff face at the same time to see who reached the top first.

Zeus and Ares held a swimming race in a nearby lake.

Apollo turned to his twin sister, Artemis.

"Obviously, you and I need to have another archery contest," he said.

"You pick the time and place, and I'll be there," Artemis replied. "This time, maybe we could try something different from our usual 'who can hit a target on a tree from the farthest distance.'"

"Oh yeah, like what?" Apollo asked.

"Maybe I can help," said a voice from behind them.

Apollo and Artemis turned around and saw Boreas, the God of the North Wind.

"I just got back from an intense training session with Poseidon," Boreas explained. He pointed to a tall mountain in the distance. The peak of the mountain was hidden by clouds.

"He took me to the top of that mountain," Boreas continued. "Once I was up there, I used my power to control the winds to create shapes and formations with clouds. It really helped me learn to focus my power."

"So, what's your idea for the archery contest?" asked Apollo.

"I can use my wind power to lift targets into the air," Boreas replied. "Then, between you and Artemis, we'll see who can hit more moving targets."

Apollo scratched his head and groaned,
but before he could say a word, Artemis
spoke.

"I'm in," she said confidently, knowing
that her brother wouldn't back down once
she agreed to the contest. "Let's start."

Apollo smirked. "Okay, then. Let's
start."

As each contest took place, Hermes busily scribbled notes on a scroll of parchment paper with the pointy end of a bird feather dipped into a stone bowl of ink.

Boreas took a deep breath, then he lifted his arms above his head and exhaled. A gust of wind whipped up, lifting a nearby fallen tree branch off the ground. The branch spun through the air.

"Target number one!" Boreas shouted.

Apollo loaded an arrow, drew back his bow, and fired. The arrow shot through the air and struck the branch as it twisted in the wind.

"Your turn!" Apollo said to his sister.

Artemis loaded her bow and aimed into the sky. The branch, with Apollo's arrow now stuck in it, swirled in the air above.

"If you insist," said Artemis, releasing her arrow. It zipped through the air and hit the branch right next to Apollo's arrow.

Dropping the tree branch, Boreas whipped up another gust of wind. This time, an apple popped off a tree and rose high into the air.

"Target number two!" shouted Boreas.

Apollo fired. His arrow struck the apple, slicing off a small chunk, before falling back to the ground.

"I hit it!" he boasted.

"Uh-huh," Artemis said softly, raising her own bow. She fired and her arrow went right through the center of the apple, slicing it into two equal-sized pieces. "Hungry? Well, now we can each eat half an apple."

"Target number three!" Boreas shouted as he used his powers to lift a single leaf off the ground and into the air.

"You'll never hit this one," Apollo said to Artemis. "It's too small and it's moving too fast."

Apollo emphasized his point by raising his right hand, accidentally releasing the next arrow he had set up. The arrow flew off and struck a nearby tree.

Remaining calm, Artemis fired her arrow and shredded the leaf as the tiny pieces whipped through the air.

"You missed, Apollo, and Artemis hit the target," Boreas stated. "She wins!"

Artemis smiled calmly and looked over at Hermes, who was taking notes.

"She's right, Apollo," Hermes said. "You missed and Artemis did not. The *Eureka News* will report her as the winner."

"Big deal," said Apollo, sulking as he picked up the apple Artemis had cut in two and took a bite out of it. "The only reason I lost is that I didn't want to beat my sister so badly. She would just stay quiet and mope, like she's always done since we were little kids. You know, Artemis, even mom and dad knew I was a better shot than you!"

Artemis turned quickly and silently walked off into the woods.

CHAPTER 3

SIBLING SITUATIONS

With her bow and quiver of arrows slung across her shoulder, Artemis walked deep into the forest. Although she was not going to show the others how she felt, Apollo's words really stung. They always did.

As she walked, her mind flashed back to her childhood. . . .

Suddenly she was four years old again, in her childhood home on Mount Olympus with her parents: Jupiter the Titan, her dad, and Leto the Titan, her mom.

And of course, her twin brother, Apollo, was right there, too.

Artemis recalled being at the seashore with her parents and her brother. She and Apollo were building two sandcastles, side by side.

28

"Why don't you two work on a sandcastle together?" Leto asked.

"Work with *her*?" scoffed Apollo. "Why? I can build a better castle by myself."

"You think so, do you?" Artemis shot back. "Well, wait until you see what I made."

"Artemis!" Jupiter scolded her. "How many times do I have to tell you not to brag?"

"But mine *is* better!" Artemis cried, pointing at her elaborate sandcastle, complete with turrets and a moat of water surrounding it. Apollo's castle was nowhere near as elaborate. "I'm just proud of my work."

"It's fine to be pleased with your achievements, honey," said Leto. "But boasting is not a very attractive trait."

"But it was Apollo who said that he could build a better castle without me first!" Artemis pointed out.

"Oh, Artemis," said Jupiter. "Boys do that sometimes. It doesn't mean anything. Just try to be nice to your brother, okay?"

Artemis then remembered a footrace she and Apollo once had. The twins dashed across a grassy field. The race was close, but Apollo won by a stride.

"Oh, yeah!" he boasted. "I'm the fastest. I'm the fastest!"

"You certainly are," said Jupiter. "In fact, I doubt that there is a young god anywhere who is faster."

"So, it's okay for him to brag, but not me?" Artemis whined.

"He's proven that he's the fastest," Leto said. "You must learn to be gracious in defeat."

Artemis said nothing.

As she walked farther into the woods, Artemis remembered one more incident. She recalled the time that she and Apollo had a discus-throwing competition.

Apollo went first. He spun around and around, then released the discus. It cut through the air and landed a long distance away.

"Nice one!" said Leto.

Artemis went next. She spun and threw her discus. Her throw landed several feet farther than Apollo's.

"I win!" Artemis shouted.

"Well, I'm still stronger than you'll ever be!" Apollo said.

"That may be, but my form is better, and that's why I won," said Artemis.

"What did we say about boasting, Artemis?" asked Jupiter.

"That it's okay for Apollo, but not for me!" Artemis shouted at her father. Then she stormed away.

I guess the lesson is: I just have to do my best and keep my mouth shut, no matter what my stupid brother says, she recalled thinking at the time.

As she walked through the woods at Eureka, she thought: *Some things haven't changed.*

"Artemis!"

A voice suddenly rang out, shaking Artemis out of her memories. Aphrodite came running up to her.

"Are you okay?" Aphrodite asked. "I know that Apollo can be a little too competitive at times."

Artemis snorted. "Tell me something I *don't* know."

"Well, come on back," said Aphrodite. "Hermes wants to interview you. He's just about ready to finish up the very first edition of the *Eureka News*!"

CHAPTER 4

READ ALL ABOUT IT

The next morning as the young gods gathered in the dining hall for breakfast, Hermes rushed in excitedly. In his hand, he held the very first issue of the *Eureka News*.

"Here it is!" Hermes announced as he unfurled the parchment scroll. It unrolled along the table and all the young gods gathered around to read it.

"It's got an article about our petteia game, Artemis," said Athena. "Hermes accurately reports that you beat me to become Eureka's new petteia champion!"

"Thank you, Athena," said Artemis. Then she glanced over at Apollo. "It's nice to know that at least someone here can be a gracious loser."

Apollo grunted and looked away.

"Well, here's something else you can be gracious about, Apollo," said Ares. "This article about my beating you at arm wrestling. And look, you even admit that I have bigger muscles than you!"

"I still say my elbow slipped," Apollo muttered under his breath.

"It doesn't matter," said Ares. "A loss is a loss."

Aphrodite pointed at the scroll. "In case I hadn't mentioned it," she said, "this article correctly states that I found the quickest route up that big cliff and beat Athena to the top in our climbing competition," said Aphrodite.

"I think you might have said something about that once or twice," said Athena, smiling.

"And this one reports on how I beat Ares in a swimming race," said Zeus.

"Yeah," said Ares. "How did you manage that?"

"Must be all the swimming lessons Poseidon gave me when I was a little kid," Zeus replied.

"Where's the part about my archery competition with Apollo?" Artemis asked.

Hermes pointed to a long story in the middle of the scroll.

"Right here," he said, "in all its glorious detail."

Artemis picked up the scroll and as she read the article, her brow started to furrow.

"Hey, Hermes," she said. "What's the deal with this story?"

"What do you mean?" Hermes asked.

Artemis started reading aloud from the article:

"Even though Boreas created difficult-to-hit moving targets, Apollo matched every shot, no matter how small the target or how fast it was moving. He brimmed with the confidence of a true master, impressing all.

"'It took all my focus to hit those targets, but my steely eyes and steady hands helped me succeed,' said Apollo, brashly chewing on the very apple he had hit in midair."

"So?" asked Hermes.

"*So?*" Artemis repeated, hardly able to believe what she was hearing. "So you barely mentioned that I was even there, much less the fact that I WON! Did you think that Apollo was the only one in the competition? Did I suddenly turn invisible?"

"Come on, Artemis. I didn't mean anything," Hermes said. "It's just that Apollo's comments are so colorful. They make for a great story."

"'Colorful,' huh?" said Artemis, tossing the scroll onto the table. "Colorful."

She turned and headed toward the door.

"I guess that's the new word for 'bragging,'" she muttered to herself as she stormed out of the dining hall.

JUMPS AND PIES

CHAPTER 5

Later that day, the young gods were busy practicing long jumps. Following the ancient Greek tradition, the jumpers held stone weights in each hand. They swung the weights back and forth to gain momentum and increase the length of their jumps.

Artemis sat silently and watched. *Am I asking too much to just want the stories Hermes writes to tell the full truth?* she wondered.

Hestia, Goddess of the Family and Hearth, joined the group.

"What's everyone doing?" she asked.

"Zeus and Ares are teaching everyone how to do the long jump," explained Apollo. "And Hermes, here, is taking notes for the next issue of his newspaper, the *Eureka News*."

"Sounds like fun," said Hestia. "I'd love to learn how to long jump."

Hermes looked up from scribbling on his scroll and frowned.

"I don't think Hestia should waste her time learning how to long jump," he said.

"Why not?" asked Athena.

"Well, everyone here loves Hestia's fig and honey pies, right?" Hermes asked.

"Especially you," said Athena, smiling as she recalled using Hermes's love for the pies to distract him long enough to beat him in a race.

"Yeah," Hermes agreed. "So, if Hestia is here, who's going to make the fig and honey pies for all of us to enjoy later?"

Artemis stood up suddenly.

"If you want fig and honey pies so much, Hermes, why don't you go and make them yourself!" she said sternly.

Hermes was shocked. "Well, I, um . . ."

Zeus, Ares, and especially Apollo were all surprised. They had never seen Artemis get upset or show anyone else that she was angry before.

Hermes continued, "It's just that I couldn't possibly make the pies even half as good as Hestia."

"That's not the point," said Athena. "The point is, maybe you should try to learn a new skill, like Hestia is trying to do here, instead of waiting for someone else to do things for you."

"And you could even write a story about your experience learning to bake pies for that, that *newspaper* of yours," Artemis added. "In fact, I'll go ahead and write the story myself for the paper."

The whole group was stunned for a moment. None of them had ever seen Artemis act this way.

"Well, sis," Apollo said. "*This* I have to see."

And so, Artemis and Apollo joined Hermes and headed off to the large kitchen area near the back of the young gods' bunkhouse. They did not want to miss the chance to watch Hermes attempt to learn how to bake his favorite pie.

READY, SET, JUMP!

Ares, Zeus, Athena, Aphrodite, and Hestia gathered around the long, narrow pit of sand used for long jumps.

Zeus stood at one end of the pit.

"Why don't we show you how to do it first, then you can try?" Zeus said to Hestia.

"I'd like that, thanks," Hestia replied.

Zeus gripped two stones with carved stone handles and bent his knees. Then he swung his arms forward and back, again and again. On a forward swing of his arms, he leapt. Zeus soared through the air, tucking his knees into his chest. He landed about twenty feet away in the sand pit.

"Wow!" said Hestia. "It almost looked like you were flying."

"Great jump, Zeus!" said Aphrodite. "My turn!"

She picked up the stone weights and crouched at the end of the pit. She started swinging her arms. Then, with a forward thrust of her arms, she jumped, landing about fifteen feet away.

"That's fun!" she said, standing up and brushing off the sand. "It did kind of feel like flying . . . for a short distance anyway. Who's next?"

"I think the reigning Eureka arm wrestling champ should take a crack at this," said Ares.

He lined up at the end of the pit and picked up the stone weights. He swung his arms and jumped. Ares landed three feet farther than Zeus.

"Oh, yeah. It's all in the arms!" he said.

Zeus turned to Hestia.

"Don't worry about how far you go," Zeus said. "Just have fun. Let's start you out with some light weights." He handed two smaller stones with carved handles to Hestia.

"I'm not very strong," Hestia said, sounding worried. "Do you think I'll be able to do this?"

"Sure," Athena said, glancing over at Ares. "It's not just about strength. It's about proper form and using the hand weights to your advantage. Line your feet up at the start of the sand pit and bend your knees. Hold the weights tightly and start swinging your arms back and forth from your shoulders. When you are ready to jump, swing your arms forward and push off with your feet."

"Okay, but it doesn't sound as easy as making a pie," Hestia said, smiling.

She stepped to the end of the jumping pit. Then she swung her arms back and forth. She leapt, landing about ten feet into the sand pit.

"Great!" said Zeus. "Excellent first jump."

"Nice form," added Aphrodite.

"That *was* fun!" said Hestia. "And I think I did pretty well."

"You did," said Zeus.

"Too bad Hermes isn't here to write about my latest victory!" said Ares.

"Hmm . . . I wonder if Hermes is doing as well baking pies as Hestia is doing at jumping," said Athena.

A HALF-BAKED IDEA?

Meanwhile, in the kitchen area near the back of the bunkhouse, Artemis, Apollo, and Hermes were busy pulling ingredients off the pantry shelves. They were getting ready to try to make some fig and honey pies.

"I'll chop these up," said Apollo, grabbing a handful of fresh, juicy figs and a sharp knife. He chopped the figs into tiny pieces.

"I've got the honey," said Artemis. She placed a large vat of honey onto the long stone worktable.

Hermes took a big wooden spoonful of honey and started to put it into a ceramic mixing bowl. Some of the gooey honey dripped onto his hands.

"You can't make pie without butter and flour," said Artemis. "And you'll need eggs to make an egg wash for the crust. I watched my parents bake enough pies to know that."

"Right," said Hermes, turning around and starting to run—just as Apollo arrived with a bowl full of eggs. The two crashed into each other and eggs went flying into the air.

"Don't worry, I got this!" shouted Hermes.

Using his great speed, he zipped around the room, catching eggs. Every time he got one, he softly tossed it to Artemis, who gently put them back into the bowl.

Wanting to help stop the eggs from hitting the floor, Apollo reached out to catch an egg. He grabbed one, then closed his hand, crushing the egg in his fist. Sticky, slimy egg white and yolk dripped through his fingers.

"The egg wash is supposed to be for the pies!" joked Hermes.

"You know, not every problem can be solved with strength," Artemis pointed out, handing her brother a cloth.

"Yeah, I see that now," Apollo said, wiping his hand.

Hermes reached up to a high shelf and grabbed a sack of flour. He plopped it down onto the worktable and a puffy cloud shot up into the air, covering his whole head in white.

Artemis tried to hide a smile as she scribbled notes onto parchment.

"This is going to make a great story for your newspaper, Hermes," she said.

"But I haven't even started baking yet!" he cried. "I think a good story should focus on the most important facts."

"Oh, you mean like who actually won a competition, rather than who bragged the loudest during it?" Artemis said, turning to look right at Apollo.

As Hermes got to work mixing all the pie ingredients together, he looked over at Artemis.

"Are you mad at me?" he asked, stirring the flour and butter together.

"I'm not mad," said Artemis. "It just feels really, really lousy to be overlooked when you do something good."

Her thoughts turned back to her childhood competitions with Apollo again. She recalled once more how her parents always seemed to favor him no matter who did better at something. And she thought about how she chose to stay silent, even when she knew she was right.

"But it wasn't on purpose," Hermes explained. "I wasn't trying to make you feel bad."

"That doesn't really matter," said Artemis as Hermes mixed the chopped figs with the honey. "How would you feel if someone wrote a story about how the city of Argos was saved by an army of soldiers—which is true—but then never mentioned the fact that your speed and courage was what helped them save the day?"

"That would be wrong," said Hermes.

He turned and added several pieces of wood to the blazing fire in the oven.

"But the facts would be *right*," Artemis pointed out. "Just not *complete*."

Hermes grew silent as he shaped pie crusts into round, metal tins.

"Just think about it," said Artemis, jotting down more notes for her story.

A NEW STORY

The blazing wood fire in the oven crackled and popped. Hermes beat several eggs together, then added a little water to create an egg wash. He brushed the egg wash onto the crusts to add shine and color.

The pies were finally ready to be baked.

Dough for the crusts oozed over the edges of the metal pie pans. Honey dripped onto the worktable.

"Well, they aren't perfect, but the first pies I ever made are finally ready to go into the oven!" Hermes said excitedly.

He placed his pies onto a large wooden pallet.

"Here goes," he said, slowly guiding the pallet into the oven and gently sliding the pies off.

"They're in!" he shouted with glee.

"Congratulations," said Artemis.

"Well, let's see how they look and taste when they come out before you congratulate me," Hermes said.

"It doesn't really matter," Artemis replied. "The fact that you tried something you had never done before is newsworthy enough."

She jotted down a few more notes.

"Be sure to mention that some of the pies are lopsided," said Apollo.

Hermes and Artemis both turned and glared at him.

"Kidding! Just kidding!" Apollo said, holding up his hands.

"Artemis, I think I owe you an apology," Hermes said. "You're right. It wasn't fair to focus on Apollo in my article when you were the one who won the contest. I'm sorry."

"Thanks," said Artemis.

"Can I ask you why you didn't just speak up for yourself at the time?" Hermes asked.

"I think *I* can answer that one," Apollo said. "Growing up, I think our parents weren't always fair to Artemis. I realized that they liked to praise me when I did something good, and they didn't do the same for her. And maybe it went to my head, so I started bragging a little—"

"A little?" Artemis said.

"All right, bragging *a lot*. But that doesn't mean that *I* don't think you are as good as me, or better at . . . well, at pretty much everything. And besides, I can only brag about these things because of you. You drove me to try to get better because of how good you were at everything. And now if I'm really good at most things, it's because I learned it from you!"

Artemis stared at Apollo. *Can this actually be my vain twin brother showing some understanding of what I went through growing up?*

"All right," said Artemis, smiling. "Who are you, and what have you done with my brother?"

"Joking aside, Apollo is right," said Hermes. "You should try to feel more comfortable talking about your accomplishments if you want to. It's easy for Apollo."

"And for you, Hermes," Apollo added.

"And for me," Hermes admitted. "And I hope you'll be kind when you write about my pie-making."

Artemis turned back to writing her story, but she couldn't stop thinking about her brother's words.

The smell of warm figs and honey drifted from the oven and filled the kitchen. Soon, the pies were ready.

"Now we'll see how I did," said Hermes.

He slid the wooden pallet into the oven and pulled out the steaming pies. They were a bit lopsided. Brown crust hung over some of the pie tins. Steaming globs of honey dripped over the edges. But they were still pies nonetheless.

"I think in order to finish my article accurately, all of our friends need to sample these pies," said Artemis, rolling up her parchment and putting it aside for a moment.

When the pies had cooled enough, each of the young gods grabbed one and they all headed back to the jumping pit.

THE PROOF IS IN THE EATING

Artemis, Apollo, and Hermes arrived back at the jumping pit, their arms full of the pies Hermes baked. They got there just in time to see Hestia launch herself into the air. She landed a fifteen-foot jump, her personal best.

"Wow!" said Hermes. "It didn't take you long to get good at that."

"She is good, isn't she?" said Zeus. "And look, I drew a picture of Hestia jumping. Maybe you can use it in the paper." He held up a sheet of parchment with a rough sketch on it.

"Good idea," said Hermes, staring at Zeus's drawing and twisting his head to try to figure out exactly what he was looking at.

Hestia smiled as she stood up and brushed sand from herself.

"I owe you an apology," Hermes said to her. "It was wrong of me to try to keep you from learning something new just so you could make pies for us. And obviously, you are really good at the long jump!"

"Well, it looks like you won't need me to make pies for you anymore," Hestia said, looking around at what her friends held in their hands. "Those all look pretty good."

"They are a little funky around the edges," said Ares, unable to stop himself from giving Hermes a hard time.

"I don't recall *you* baking any pies, Ares," said Athena, as Ares, Zeus, Athena, and Aphrodite all gathered around Hermes, Artemis, and Apollo.

"Well, they sure smell good," said Aphrodite, who held a parchment and feather pen.

"Have you been writing an article for the *Eureka News*, too?" Artemis asked Aphrodite, pulling out her own parchment scroll.

"I have," said Aphrodite. "I wrote down all the details about the long jump competition."

"Nice," said Artemis. "I wrote up the story of Hermes learning to bake pies."

"And I'm happy to have two new reporters for the *Eureka News*," said Hermes, "but now . . . doesn't anybody want to try my pies?!"

Hermes's friends looked all around, pretending they hadn't heard him.

"Nobody?" Hermes whined.

The young gods all burst out laughing.

"I think I should be the first one to try your pies," said Hestia.

"It's only right," said Hermes.

Hestia scooped a piece of pie from the tin and took a big bite.

"Pretty good for your first try," she said to Hermes. "I'm happy to give you some baking tips if you like—and a few long jumping tips, too!"

Hermes smiled. Then everyone grabbed a piece of pie.

"This is good!" said Zeus through a mouthful of gooey fig and honey.

The others all agreed.

"Hey, Hermes," said Artemis. "You haven't even tasted your own pie!"

"I'm a little nervous," Hermes admitted.

"The great Hermes, nervous?" said Artemis. "I can hardly believe it."

"All right, all right," Hermes said, waving off his friends. "Here goes nothing."

Hermes took a bite of one of his pies. His face scrunched up a little.

"Hestia, I may just take you up on your offer of baking tips," he said.

"Does that mean you don't like it?" Hestia asked as she took another mouthful.

"Let's just say it's not as good as your pies," Hermes replied.

"Breaking news!" Aphrodite announced, writing on her scroll. "Hermes admits he isn't the best at something! This will make a great article for tomorrow's paper."

"Yeah, yeah, alright. I guess I deserved that," said Hermes. "But it doesn't mean I won't try again."

Hermes took another mouthful of pie.

"So, Aphrodite, Artemis," he said. "Since I'm going to have to practice my baking and won't have as much time to devote to the newspaper, would you both like to be my co-editors?"

"Sure!" said Aphrodite.

"I'm in," added Artemis.

"Well, we better get busy, then," said Aphrodite, taking one more quick bite of pie. "The *Eureka News* is not going to publish itself!"

CHAPTER 10

THE EUREKA NEWS

The next morning, the young gods all gathered for breakfast. Hermes unrolled the latest edition of the *Eureka News*. They all began to read:

Zeus

PIE LOVER LEARNS TO BAKE

By Artemis

A big-time fan of Hestia's fig and honey pies, Hermes took a bold step toward being able to eat more pies: He decided to learn how to bake these pies himself. With Apollo and this reporter watching (full disclosure, we also helped a bit), the well-known speedster attacked the challenge with energy and daring.

Following a few messy mishaps— including airborne eggs, puffs of flour, and droopy dough—Hermes proved himself able to learn a new skill, while remaining humble enough to admit that he needed more practice.

"Running always came naturally to me," said Hermes. "But baking . . . well, baking is going to take some more work to perfect. But, I think that I'm up to the challenge."

I know that everyone at Eureka wishes him luck and looks forward to enjoying the "fruits" of his labor. In other words, more pie for everybody!

BAKER TAKES
GIANT LEAP FORWARD
By Aphrodite

Best known for her skill in the kitchen, Hestia, Goddess of Family and Hearth, surprised her Eureka family by announcing that she wanted to learn how to long jump.

Hestia, though a bit nervous at first, showed determination as she learned the proper techniques—how to grip the stone weights that help jumpers go farther, how to swing her arms back and forth to build up momentum so the jump is longer, and how to land safely.

"I was pretty nervous at first," admitted Hestia. "But all the other gods here were so helpful and supportive, I felt comfortable trying. My goal now is to break Ares's record of a twenty-three-foot jump."

I have no doubt that, given time and practice, Hestia will soon be challenging Ares for the Eureka long jumping championship.

GOD OF THE WEEK

By Hermes

As the Editor-in-Chief of the *Eureka News*, I am pleased to announce a new feature—God of the Week. Each week, we will feature a god who has done a fantastic feat that deserves recognition. I imagine that in the future, I'll be writing about great deeds of strength or speed or smarts or excellence in athletic competition. But for our first God of the Week, the achievement I'm going to write about takes a different form.

I'm happy to announce that the *Eureka News's* first God of the Week is Artemis, the Archer. Her skill with a bow is well-known and unmatched. But the reason we are celebrating Artemis as our God of the Week is because of something else. It's about her character.

We all know Artemis as a quiet god. She goes about her business and always displays skill, bravery, and heroics. But her quiet personality can work against her. She doesn't boast or brag about her achievements, she just continues to excel. But sometimes, because of her nature, she remains silent even when she feels that she has been wronged.

All that changed this week. In the very first issue of the *Eureka News,* I wrote an article about the archery competition between Artemis and her twin brother, Apollo. And in this article, I hardly mentioned Artemis. That was my mistake, and it might have gone unnoticed and uncorrected, except that this time, Artemis chose to speak up. She pointed out that despite her achievement, she was unhappy that her victory went unsung. Well, no more. Artemis is our first God of the Week because she stood up for herself and spoke out for what is right.

Oh, and to set the record straight, Artemis soundly beat Apollo in the archery contest.

Congratulations to our God of Week!

Read on for a sneak peek of . . .

THE ALIEN NEXT DOOR

THE NEW KID

BY A. I. NEWTON   ILLUSTRATED BY ANJAN SARKAR   1

From the creators
of Little Olympians!

THE NEW SCHOOL

THE NEW KID SAT ALONE IN

the back of the bus. He was on his way to his first day at a new school.

Once again.

He watched as the other kids fooled around. They giggled and yelled. No one else seemed to be just sitting in their seat.

Except him. The new kid.

Once again.

Taking this "bus" thing to school with everyone else is really dumb, he thought. Back home we got to school on our own. And much faster than in this clunky yellow hunk of metal. And instead of messing around the whole way like these kids, we had time to think and prepare for learning. But this . . .

The new kid shook his head. No one on the bus seemed to even notice that he was there.

Here we go again, he thought. *Will anyone like me? Will I make any friends? Why do my parents have to move so much?*

The new boy sighed. He knew why they were always moving. They were research scientists. Their work took them from place to place. And every time they moved, he had to start over in a new school. He had to make new friends. He had to learn how things were done in a new place.

"Hey, Charlie!" one kid shouted at his friend. "Did you finish last week's homework?"

"I finished it this morning," another kid shouted back. "Right on time!"

The bus rocked with laughter.

The new kid didn't understand. What was funny about waiting until the last minute to do your schoolwork? He didn't like always feeling different. He was tired of being the strange new kid once again.

And he missed his home.

I have friends back home. I know how stuff works there. All of this is so . . . different, so strange.

The bus slowed to a stop and the doors opened. The kids bounded down the stairs and ran toward the school.

The new kid got out of his seat. He walked slowly to the front of the bus to exit.

"Good luck today," said the bus driver. She smiled warmly at him. It made him feel a little better.

Here I go again, he thought. Then he took a deep breath, walked into the school, and hoped for the best.